You are Divine

by
Biruh Alemayehu Woldearegay

illustrated by
Victoria Mikki

Biblical Affirmations for Children

Book design by Victoria Mikki
Text by Biruh Alemayehu Woldearegay

First Printing: August 2022

Visit www.identityempowered.com

This book is dedicated to my daughters Liyou, Misgana, and Melkam.
May you continue to grow in knowing who you are in Christ and see
yourself as God sees you — chosen, worthy, victorious, beautiful, honored,
and so much more. In a world full of lies, doubt, and confusion, may you
always find your way back to the word of truth, which is the living
Word of God.

I will always love and guide you every step of the way.

Train up a child in the way he should go;
even when he is old, he will not depart from it.
— Proverbs 22:6

ACKNOWLEDGMENTS

First and foremost, glory to God for His grace and guidance in getting this book out to the world. This book is from Him, through Him, and for Him.

To my amazing husband and best friend, Sasibeh Beyene (Babi): Thank you for supporting me through the journey of becoming a published author. Thank you for always believing in my wildest dreams and never-ending creative ideas. You are the backbone of this project and none of this would have been possible without your support and encouragement. I am beyond grateful to experience this life with you.
I love you!

To my parents, sister, and close friends who have believed and prayed for this project: Thank you all for your support and encouragement. Having an idea and turning it into a book was both challenging and rewarding at the same time. Thank you for giving me your ears when I was excited to share every milestone and when I needed to vent out of frustration, especially when I had done all the hard work but simply couldn't come up with a title. I am blessed to have you all in my life.

To the most talented and creative illustrator, Victoria Mikki: Thank you for bringing my ideas to life. You nailed every illustration and have exceeded my expectation!

To Mandi Summit at Red Quill LLC: Without your editing service, this book would not have turned out the way it did. Thank you for your exceptional service, professionalism, and generosity. I look forward to working with you on future projects.

To J. Nicole Starnes at Jot & Tittle: A Proofreading Service LLC: Thank you for looking over the final manuscript and affirming to me that this book will not only bless little ones but also adult readers of faith.

Finally, a very special thanks to Adian Barada Bell: Thank you for helping me discover my inner love and passion for books. I will always cherish our stories during mealtime and how you would beg me to keep reading you books as you played with Thomas the Train, James, Percy, Sir Topham Hatt, and Gordon, to name a few. You will always have a special place in my life.

*Jesus said, "Let the little children come to me,
and do not hinder them, for the Kingdom of Heaven
belongs to such as these."*
—Matthew 19:14

You Are Fearfully and Wonderfully Made

The patterns on your fingerprints,
Freckles on your skin,
The color of your eyes,
And the dimples on your chin:

Each of these designed
By your Heavenly Father.
Have confidence, dear child,
For God is your creator.

DIVINE TRUTH

You are perfectly made in the image of God.
He took His time when He formed you in your mother's womb.

Designed – to make or plan // **Confidence** – to trust or have faith //
Divine – Godlike or heavenly

God's Word
I praise you because I am fearfully and wonderfully made;
your works are wonderful, I know that full well.
—Psalm 139:14

Let's Discuss
What is one thing you love about your body and why?

Provide – to supply what is needed // **Royalty** – a member of a royal family (king, queen, princess, prince)

You Are a Child of God

God is your Father in heaven
Who cares and watches over you.
He provides for your needs
And loves you through and through.

So, if anyone asks who you are,
Tell them loud and proud:
You are a child of the most-high God,
Of Him up there in the clouds.

DIVINE TRUTH

You are royalty, princess and prince,
For you belong to God, the King of kings.

God's Word

See what great love the Father has lavished on us, that we should be called children of God! And that is what we are! The reason the world does not know us is that it did not know Him.
—1 John 3:1

Let's Discuss

How can you strengthen your relationship with God as your Heavenly Father?

You Are Loved

To prove His love to you,
He gave His only son.
The perfect Lamb of God
Who is the only one.

Upon that weary cross
Through Jesus's sacrifice,
You can live eternal,
For the Savior paid the price.

DIVINE TRUTH

The love God has for you is unconditional.
He loves you even more than your own mother and father.
Isn't that amazing?

Unconditional – without limit // **Sacrifice** – the act of giving up something of great value to show deep affection // **Eternal** – lasting always and forever // **Savior** – someone who saves

God's Word

For God so loved the world that He gave His one and only Son, that whoever believes in Him shall not perish but have eternal life.
—John 3:16

Let's Discuss

How can you share the love God has for you with others?

You Are Strong

You are a child of God.
There is nothing you can't do.
You are made to conquer,
For God lives in you.

At times, you may face challenges
And get discouraged a bit.
Whenever things get hard,
Always pray and never quit.

DIVINE TRUTH

Who says you can't handle tough things?
If you believe in God, tough times will only make you stronger.

Conquer – to win // **Discouraged** –
to lose hope or confidence

God's Word
I can do all this through Him who gives me strength.
—Philippians 4:13

Let's Discuss
What are some difficult
things you can do with
the help of God?

You Have a Purpose

Come one and come all!
Light skin or darker tone,
Young or old, short or tall,
You have a purpose that is known.

An artist, a doctor, a singer, or a writer.
Whatever it is that you aspire,
God knows your future,
And He holds your heart's desire.

DIVINE TRUTH

You may not know what your future holds,
But believe in your heart that you are destined for greatness.

Purpose – a plan that guides an action // **Aspire** – to have
a great desire for something // **Desire** – to want or wish for

God's Word

"For I know the plans I have for you," declares the Lord, "plans to prosper you and not to harm you, plans to give you hope and a future."
—Jeremiah 29:11

Let's Discuss

What do you aspire to become when you grow up, and how can God use your talents for His Kingdom?

God Is Always with You

God says He is Immanuel,
Which means He's always with you.
He will help, comfort, and strengthen,
No matter what you go through.

As you feel His presence,
Let your heart begin to trust,
For He will take away your fear
And give you peace and rest.

DIVINE TRUTH

Do you ever feel scared or alone or that no one cares at all?
Have faith and be strong, for God is always with you.

God's Word

So do not fear, for I am with you;
do not be dismayed, for I am your God.
I will strengthen you and help you;
I will uphold you with my righteous right hand.
—Isaiah 41:10

Let's Discuss

What are some fears you can face
with the help of the Holy Spirit?

You Are Protected

You are always protected
While here on this earth.
God has surrounded you with angels
From the moment of your birth.

They will protect you from harm
As you travel each day through.
There are angels all around
Watching over me and you.

Protect – to guard against injury or destruction // **Surround** – to close off all sides

DIVINE TRUTH

Are you scared of the dark or when your parents are not around?
Fear not, you are a child protected by the most-high God!

God's Word

*For He will command His angels concerning you
to guard you in all your ways;
they will lift you up in their hands,
so that you will not strike your foot against a stone.*
—Psalm 91:11–12

Let's Discuss

What are some things God can protect you from?

You Are Forgiven

You may have disobeyed your parents,
Stolen, cheated, or told a few lies.
But the moment you confess your sins,
You are forgiven in God's eyes.

And because you have the Holy Spirit,
Your Helper in times of need,
You can also forgive others
Who have broken, hurt, or bullied.

DIVINE TRUTH

We all make mistakes from time to time,
But God forgives us when we
confess our sins.

Confess – to admit as true // **Sin** – to do something against God's law

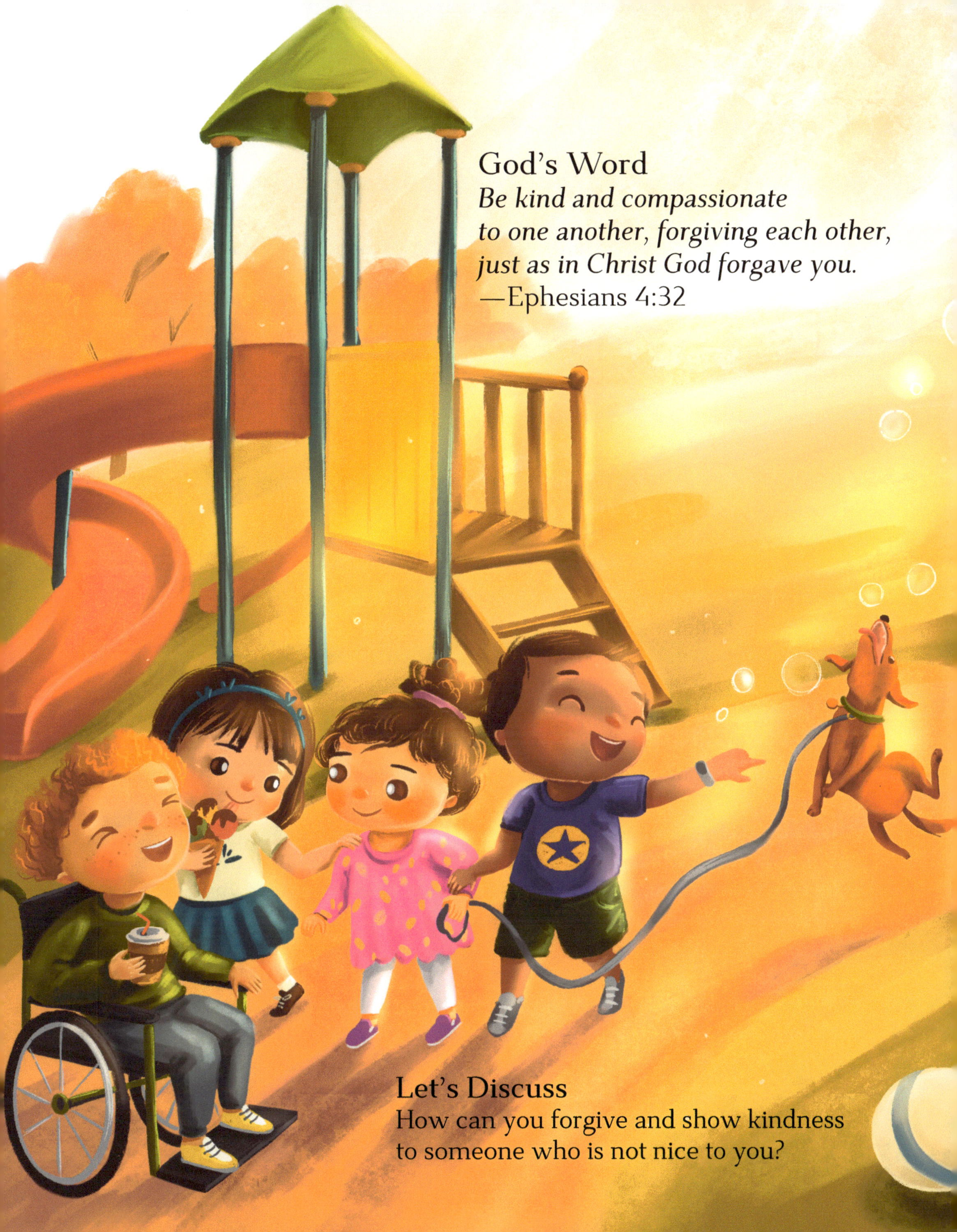

God's Word
Be kind and compassionate
to one another, forgiving each other,
just as in Christ God forgave you.
—Ephesians 4:32

Let's Discuss
How can you forgive and show kindness
to someone who is not nice to you?

Bible scriptures on Identity

- **John 1:12**
  Yet to all who did receive him, to those who believed in his name, he gave the right to become children of God –

- **2 Corinthians 5:17**
  Therefore, if anyone is in Christ, the new creation has come: The old has gone, the new is here!

- **Psalm 100:3**
  Know that the Lord is God. It is he who made us, and we are his; we are his people, the sheep of his pasture.

- **1 Peter 2:9**
  But you are a chosen people, a royal priesthood, a holy nation, God's special possession, that you may declare the praises of him who called you out of darkness into his wonderful light.

- **Ephesians 1:4**
  For he chose us in him before the creation of the world to be holy and blameless in his sight. In love.

- **Isaiah 43:1**
  But now, this is what the Lord says—he who created you, Jacob, he who formed you, Israel: "Do not fear, for I have redeemed you; I have summoned you by name; you are mine.

- **Ephesians 1:7**
  In him we have redemption through his blood, the forgiveness of sins, in accordance with the riches of God's grace.

- **Ephesians 3:12**
  In him and through faith in him we may approach God with freedom
  and confidence.

- **Isaiah 49:16**
  See, I have engraved you on the palms of my hands; your walls are ever
  before me.

- **Philippians 3:20**
  But our citizenship is in heaven. And we eagerly await a Savior from there,
  the Lord Jesus Christ.

Note to Parents and Guardians

Dear parents/guardians:

I hope you enjoyed reading this book with your little ones. I pray every affirmation brings divine confidence and truth to your child's life.
The Bible tells us that children are a gift from God and a reward from Him (Psalm 127:3–5). God has trusted us as parents to raise them in ways that they know who they are and what has been done for them through Jesus Christ.

This world is often too quick to label our children with false identities and push them to settle for less than their God-given potential and destiny.
I believe the only way we can win over this false narrative is by equipping our children with the full armor of God, which is the Word of God (Ephesians 6:10–17). When our children know who they are in Christ and have a solid anchor in the belief that they belong to God who declares that He is El-Shaddai – 'God Almighty' (Genesis 17:1 NLT), they can overcome any challenges and tough seasons that come their way.

Therefore, be encouraged to speak life and blessings unto them, encourage them to read the Bible, and help them embrace their divine identity in Christ Jesus.

Many blessings,

Biruh A. Woldearegay

www.ingramcontent.com/pod-product-compliance
Lightning Source LLC
Chambersburg PA
CBHW041416300726

48978CB00002B/114